MAXI, THE HERO

MAXI, THE HERO

by Debra and Sal Barracca
pictures by Mark Buehner

▪▫▪▫▪▫▪▫▪▫▪▫▪▫▪▫▪▫▪▫▪

A Puffin Pied Piper

PUFFIN PIED PIPER BOOKS
Published by the Penguin Group
Penguin Books USA Inc., 375 Hudson Street, New York, New York, 10014, U.S.A.
Penguin Books Ltd, 27 Wrights Lane, London W8 5TZ, England
Penguin Books Australia Ltd, Ringwood, Victoria, Australia
Penguin Books Canada Ltd, 10 Alcorn Avenue, Toronto, Ontario, Canada M4V 3B2
Penguin Books (N.Z.) Ltd, 182–190 Wairau Road, Auckland 10, New Zealand
Penguin Books Ltd, Registered Offices: Harmondsworth, Middlesex, England

Originally published in hardcover by
Dial Books for Young Readers
A member of Penguin Putnam Inc.

Text copyright © 1991 by Debra & Sal Barracca
Pictures copyright © 1991 by Mark Buehner
All rights reserved
Designed and created by Halcyon Books Inc.
Library of Congress Catalog Card Number: 90-38329
Printed in Hong Kong
First Puffin Pied Piper Printing 1994
ISBN 0-14-055497-1
A Pied Piper Book is a registered trademark of Dial Books for
Young Readers, a member of Penguin Putnam Inc.,
® TM 1,163,686 and ® TM 1,054, 312.

5 7 9 10 8 6 4

The art for this book was prepared by using oil paints over acrylics.

MAXI, THE HERO is also available in hardcover from
Dial Books for Young Readers.

To Florence Miller, a very special mom,
with much love.
D.B. and S.B.

To Merrill and Cynthia,
for your extraordinary enthusiasm.
M.B.

Jim drives a big taxi
And I'm his dog, Maxi.
Each morning we rise with the sun.
We greet our boss, Lou,
Have a biscuit or two,
Then set out to make our first run.

The day is just dawning
    And Jim is still yawning.
        We drive down the street to the pier.
There's no one around,
    And you can't hear a sound,
        But the toot of a tug that draws near.

"Can you take us uptown
     To the Hotel Crown?"
          Ask two sailors who've just come ashore.
"We sailed in from Tahiti—
     I'm Al and he's Petey."
          (Never saw a real sailor before!)

We drive up the street
  And hear a drum beat.
    We see a parade passing by!
The music's so loud
  And there's such a huge crowd
    Watching giant balloons in the sky.

It's already noon—
      Lunchtime, so soon!
            We head for Joe's frankfurter cart.
Jim always buys three,
      Two for him, one for me,
            And after, a blueberry tart.

We heard someone calling,
   "My meatballs are falling!"
      It's a chef with a tray of spaghetti!
"I'm late for a wedding,
   Across town I'm heading,
      And please try to keep the cab steady!"

Then we got quite a shock
When we drove 'round the block.
There were three boys who had the same face!
"We're triplets," they said.
"Call us Ed, Ned, and Fred.
Our ball team just took second place!"

We dropped off the boys,
    Then heard a loud noise.
        "Stop, thief!" a woman cried out.
And, in a flash,
    I made a mad dash,
        As Jim cheered me on with a shout!

A man stole her purse,
    And to make matters worse,
        All her groceries had spilled to the ground.
There were rolling tomatoes
    And bouncing potatoes,
        And peaches and pears by the pound!

The thief tried to flee—
    It was now up to me!
        I had to run faster to catch him.
I was close to his heel,
    When he slipped on a peel,
        And at last I was able to snatch him.

He gave me a fight,
But I held on so tight—
The police came along very fast.
The crowd yelled, "Hooray!"
As they led him away.
The big chase was over at last.

Next day in the paper,
They told of the caper.
My picture appeared on page one!
Jim patted my head.
"You're a hero!" he said.
"I'm proud of you, that was well done."

I loved my new fame,
    People knowing my name.
        "What a brave dog you are!" they would shout.
"That's him—there goes Maxi!
    And look, there's his taxi!"
        We'd hear as we traveled about.

As another day ends,
    We've made some new friends,
        Had lots of adventures too.
Tomorrow, there's more—
    Who knows what's in store?
        Come along, I'll be looking for you!

ABOUT THE AUTHORS

Debra and Sal Barracca are the owners of Halcyon books, in which they work with many artists and authors of children's books. After riding in a taxi whose driver kept his own dog in the cab with him, the Barraccas wrote their first book, *The Adventures of Taxi Dog* (Dial), which was also illustrated by Mark Buehner. Both native New Yorkers, the Barraccas live in Somers, New York, with their daughter and their cat.

ABOUT THE ARTIST

Mark Buehner was born and raised in Utah, and graduated from Utah State University. He has illustrated several children's books, the first of which, *The Adventures of Taxi Dog,* was a *Reading Rainbow* selection and was given a starred review by *Booklist*. Mr. Buehner lives with his wife, children, and their cat in Salt Lake City, Utah.